powerful man in the universe and the protector of Castle Grayskull. Prince Adam's pet tiger Cringer turned into the mighty Battle Cat, He-Man's faithful companion.

Only Orko, the court magician, and Man-at-Arms, He-Man's best friend, knew this secret. Even Prince Adam's parents and Teela, captain of the guard, saw him only as the prince of Eternia. Prince Adam kept his secret because danger lived on Eternia.

On one side of the planet, the sun never shined. There, inside Snake Mountain, the wicked Skeletor planned new ways to find

out Castle Grayskull's secrets. And still others with bad intentions waited on other worlds, ready to disturb Eternia's peaceful way of life.

Against them all stood only He-Man and the Masters of the Universe!

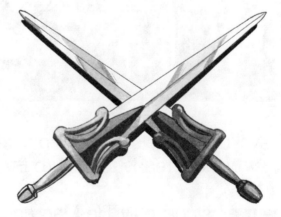

THE RIVER OF RUIN

Written by Bryce Knorr

Illustrated by Harry J. Quinn and James Holloway

Creative Direction by Jacquelyn A. Lloyd

Design Direction by Ralph E. Eckerstrom

A GOLDEN BOOK

Western Publishing Company, Inc.
Racine, Wisconsin 53404

Library of Congress Catalog Card Number 84-62346
ISBN 0-932631-03-7
A B C D E F G H I J

Classic™ Binding U.S. Patent #4,408,780
Patented in Canada 1984.
Patents in other countries issued or pending.
R. R. Donnelley and Sons Company

"Come on, Prince Adam, faster!"

Teela's jet scooter screamed over the courtyard. Behind her, Prince Adam tried to catch up.

"I-I-I can't watch," Cringer said. The scared tiger held a string for the finish line.

"You both should slow down. S-s-someone could get hur--"

Teela and Prince Adam raced neck-and-neck. Next to Cringer, a door opened. There stood King Randor with Ramjah, leader of the fishermen.

"But Ramjah," King Randor said. "Why are your people angry at the farmers? You should learn to get along together."

The king and his guest stepped into the courtyard. Teela and Prince Adam had no time to stop!

"Look out!" Teela shouted.

The racers just missed a hay wagon. The wagon swerved and hay flew everywhere!

"N-n-now you're in trouble," Cringer said. He tried to crawl away.

"Not so fast, Cringer," Man-at-Arms said. "Prince Adam and Teela need your help to clean up this mess.

"Prince Adam and Teela, take this hay to the horses. It's time you two learned to work together as a team."

"Why can't everyone get along?" King Randor asked Ramjah. "Like you and Ar-Bor, chief of the farmers. You could be friends if you tried."

"Never!" Ramjah said. He banged his spear in anger. "We fish the River of Rain. Water scares the farmers. They are not brave and strong like us!"

The hay was back on the wagon.

"Race you to the stable!" Prince Adam yelled.

"Oh, no. Here we go again," Cringer said.

But this race ended when Prince Adam saw Sy-Klone. The human tornado was worried.

"Earthquakes are shaking the Mystic Mountains," Sy-Klone said. "There are lots of them near the start of the River of Rain."

High in the Mystic Mountains, the ground shook. But earth-quakes were not the cause. This was the work of Skeletor. He laughed as Land Shark ripped into the ground.

"It's music to my ears," Skeletor said.
"Just a little more and the new river will be done. Soon the River of Rain will be a river of ruin!"

Blasts from Land Shark made huge rocks fall and block the river. The river water flowed into the new path that Skeletor dug.

"The river flows where I want it to," Skeletor said.
"Nothing can stop my plan now."

The farmers lived in the valley below the Mystic Mountains. Prince Adam and his friends flew there to learn about the earthquakes.

"Ramjah's fishermen are to blame," said Ar-Bor, chief of the farmers. "The Man in the Mountain doesn't want them fishing his river. This is his warning."

"A man in the mountain?" Teela asked:

"It's a legend," Prince Adam said.
"But the dislike between the farmers and the fishermen is no legend. It's real."

"We could fly up to the mountains," Sy-Klone said. "But there is too much fog."

Suddenly, a great roar filled the air. A tall wall of water rushed toward them!

Teela flew her Wind Raider to safety. But Prince Adam could not get to his in time.

"I have only one chance," he thought. The huge wave shadowed Prince Adam.

"By the power of Grayskull," he cried.

"I HAVE THE POWER!"

The roaring river could not stop He-Man. When he reached shore, he saw Teela searching for Prince Adam.

"Teela, over here!" He-Man yelled.

"Is Prince Adam all right?" she asked.

"He took Wind Raider to get help," He-Man answered. He hopped onto the back of Teela's flyer.

"We must help those farmers. Come on!"

He-Man, Teela and Sy-Klone teamed up for the rescue. Sy-Klone looked for those in need. Teela flew Wind Raider. He-Man pulled people out of the water.

"Thank you, He-Man," Ar-Bor said. "Our farms are under water. But we are safe. We are afraid of the water. But not even the Man in the Mountain can stop you."

"I could not have done it without my friends," He-Man said. **"But I wonder. Is the Man in the Mountain really the cause?"**
Ar-Bor answered He-Man's question several days later.
"It's a message from Ar-Bor," Sy-Klone told He-Man. "He says beasts are attacking. He thinks it's the Man in the Mountain."

"It's time to find out about this Man in the Mountain,"
He-Man said.

Once again the heroes flew to the valley. But fog still kept the mountain's secret. The valley, though, was indeed being overrun by beasts!

"The fog can't hide those beasts," Teela said.
"I've never seen so many before."

"Let's round them up,"
He-Man said.

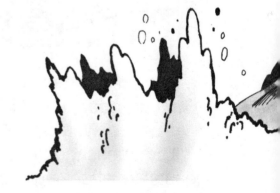

The chase was on! When the animals saw the new river, they jumped into the water and floated downstream.

"Thank you again, He-Man," Ar-Bor said. "We hope the Man in the Mountain is done. It is he who sent the beasts. But there will be more trouble if the fishermen make him angry."

"Can't you be friends with the fishermen?" He-Man asked.

"No!" Ar-Bor said. "The fishermen smell as awful as their fish. We cannot be their friends. The Man in the Mountain will hurt us."

From the bushes, a voice spoke.

"Your problem is not a man in a mountain," the voice said.

"Who speaks?" Ar-Bor asked. "I see no one."

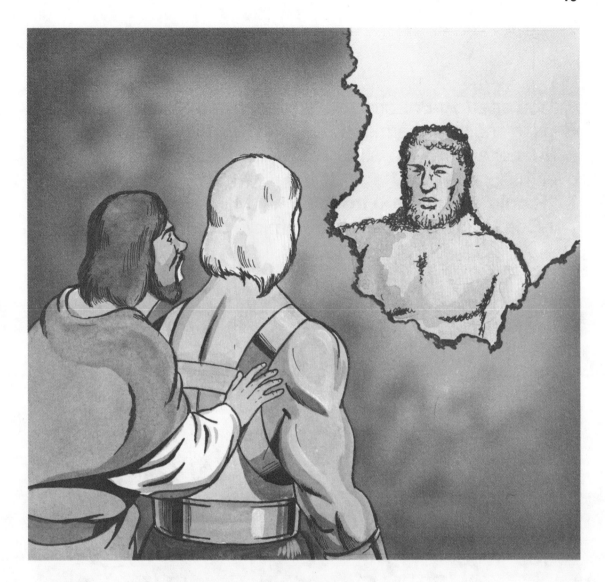

A green man stepped from the bushes.

"I am Moss Man. I can hide anywhere. I blend in among the plants and trees of the forest."

"Hello, Moss Man," He-Man said.
"I know you can tell us about those beasts."

"They followed the river here," Moss Man said. "Water is their home. The old riverbed is dry."

"You see!" Ar-Bor cried. "The Man in the Mountain punishes Ramjah and the fishermen!"

"It's not a man," Moss Man said. "It's Skeletor! His men are all over the forest."

"Ramjah could be in trouble!" He-Man said. **"Ar-Bor, I know you don't like Ramjah. But will you help us?"**

"Yes," Ar-Bor answered. "But only because you have helped us so much, He-Man."

"Good," He-Man said. **"Let's take Bashasaurus."**

Moss Man scouted ahead. He blended into the forest so well that not even the animals saw him move through the trees.

"We are close to Ramjah's village, He-Man," Moss Man said. "Something is very wrong."

They sneaked up on the village. They saw that Skeletor was making the fishermen dig a large hole.

Snakes crawled around Skeletor's feet. Kobra Khan, wicked master of snakes, looked on with a twisted smile.

"Excellent, Kobra Khan," Skeletor said.

"Snakes are the only thing I like more than doing evil."

"*Work harder!*" Skeletor yelled at Ramjah.
"*You'd better find the Eternium tomorrow. Spikor! Webstor! Chain them up for the night!*"

"**So that's Skeletor's plan,**" He-Man whispered.
"**He changed the river so he could mine Eternium, a magical source of power. With Eternium's power, Skeletor could rule all of Eternia!**"

"Only Spikor and Webstor are guarding the fishermen," Teela said. "We can give Skeletor a surprise he won't like."

Spikor and Webstor weren't watching Ramjah and his people. Instead, they were arguing.

"Let's see what the catch of the day is," Teela said.

She began to swing a net over her head.

"Watch out," Sy-Klone warned. "Don't get near Spikor's spikes."

Teela sneaked up behind Spikor. She threw the net over him.

"Hold on, Teela," Moss Man said. "I'll take care of his spikes."

Moss Man picked up a log and pushed it toward Spikor until it was stuck solidly onto Spikor's spikes. Skeletor's dangerous warrior was made helpless.

Webstor prepared to use his hook against the heroes.

"How do you like my hook, green one?" he asked. Before Webstor could use his hook against Moss Man, Ar-Bor caught it with his pitchfork. He pulled the rope away.

"It's time to give *you* the hook, Webstor,"
Sy-Klone said. The human tornado took off
with the rope. 'Round and 'round he flew.
Webstor was tied up with his own rope!

He-Man broke the chains that bound Ramjah and his people. The fishermen were free! He-Man tied the chains around Webstor and Spikor.

"Thank you, He-Man," Ramjah said. "And thank you, too, Ar-Bor. We were wrong about you. How can I help?"

"The river hurt the farmers' fields," He-Man said. **"We must get the water back there. But the fog keeps us off the mountain."**

"You need a strong wind," Ramjah said. "It always blows away the fog on the river."

"I know where to find a wind," He-Man said.
"Teela, help the others to high ground. Sy-Klone and I have a mountain to visit."

They rode Bashasaurus all night. The sun was rising when they reached the Mystic Mountains. Fog still hid the hills.

"One wind, coming right up," Sy-Klone said. The human tornado took off.

Sy-Klone's wind lifted the fog. He-Man rode Bashasaurus up the mountain. At the top, he found Skeletor's dam of rocks.

"We must knock a hole in those rocks," He-Man said. **"Stand back, Sy-Klone."**

He-Man gave the dam a super-punch. The rocks flew, but didn't fall. Sy-Klone flew into the wall. But it stood still.

"Bashasaurus can break through," He-Man said. **"But can I get it away in time?"**

He-Man rode the mighty machine toward the rocks.

"Here goes!" He-Man said. The bashing arm knocked the dam again and again.

The wall cracked. Water dripped between the stones. He-Man drove Bashasaurus out of the way and walked back to the dam.

"It needs some help," Sy-Klone said.

He-Man gave the dam his strongest *thunder punch!* This time the wall that Skeletor built fell down. A river of rocks and water washed toward He-Man.

Sy-Klone flew into the air, whirling with great speed. His wind blew the water away from He-Man.

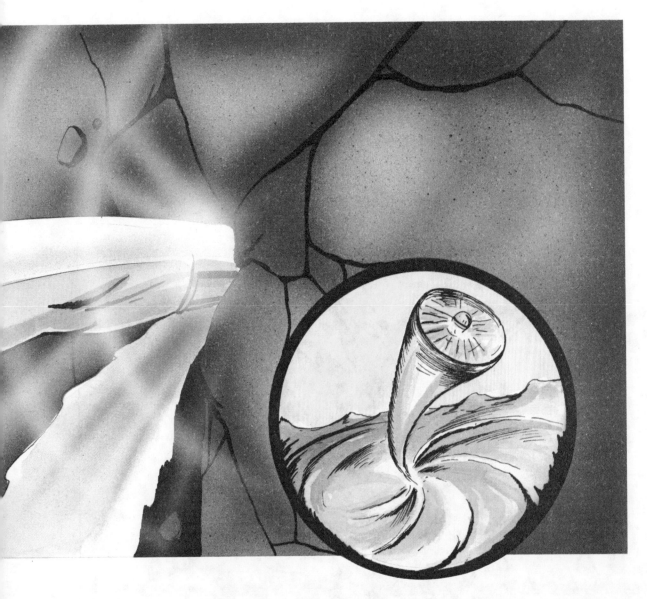

"I'll make sure the river goes where it's supposed to," Sy-Klone said. "See you at Ramjah's village!"

He-Man rode Bashasaurus down the mountain. He didn't stop until he saw Skeletor. Skeletor and his men were stuck in the mud!

"He-Man!" Skeletor yelled.
"You ruined the mine. I'll get you for this! Attack!"

Sy-Klone helped He-Man by blowing the mud all over Skeletor and his men. Skeletor was angrier than ever. He jumped on Land Shark and threatened He-Man.

"Let's just see if you think my Land Shark's bite is so funny," Skeletor said.

"**You need a bath, Skeletor,**" He-Man said. Bashasaurus' bashing arm splashed water all over Land Shark. Skeletor tried to start the machine. But it was too wet.

"**Your shark can't swim, Skeletor,**" He-Man said. "**And you are all wet, too.**"

"I'll get even with you, He-Man," Skeletor shouted.
"Come on, you fools. Push Land Shark back to Snake Mountain. I'll make Land Shark stronger than ever."

Many snakes nipped at Skeletor's men as they pushed. These snakes didn't like being cold and wet, either.

With He-Man's help, the fishermen and farmers worked together. Ramjah's people helped the farmers plant new fields. Ar-Bor's people helped the fishermen fix their village.

Finally, the work was done. They had a big party. He-Man and his friends were the special guests.

"Thank you, He-Man," Ramjah said. "Without your help, we would still be Skeletor's slaves."

"And our fields would be under water," Ar-Bor said. "Here's to He-Man. We're grateful to you."

"It wasn't just me," He-Man said.
"I could not have done it without my friends. Together we make quite a team."

"We should thank Skeletor for discovering the Eternium," He-Man said. "Man-at-Arms can show you how to mine it safely. Both villages can work the mine. Everyone can use the Eternium and put its power to good use—except Skeletor."

"Hear hear, He-Man," Man-at-Arms said. "I think Teela learned a lesson about doing things together. Didn't you, daughter?"

"Yes, I have, Father. I just wish Prince Adam were here to learn it, too," she said.

Man-at-Arms and He-Man just winked at each other.

THE END